An International I

INSPIRATIONAL UPLIF㑊㑊
WORDS FOR
MULTINATIONAL
GENERATIONS!

Forward by Ambassador
Professor, Dr. Joseph S. Spence Sr.
Epulaeryu Master!

Clever Fox
PUBLISHING

Chennai • Bangalore

CLEVER FOX PUBLISHING
Chennai, India

Published by CLEVER FOX PUBLISHING 2022
Copyright © Dr. Joseph S. Spence Sr. 2022

All Rights Reserved.
ISBN: 978-93-91537-51-7

ENDORSEMENTS

Congratulations to His Excellency, Ambassador, Dr. Joseph Spence Sr., Master of Epulaeryu Poetry, for another fantastic book, "International Family Poetry Anthology." It brings daily inspirational messages through each poem. It reforms family unity with strength, love, and togetherness. The family enjoys his inspirational books and words of wisdom written by a professional master, including *A Trilogy of Poetry, Prose, and Thoughts for the Mind, Body, and Soul* (2005). *Trilogy Moments for the Mind Body and Soul* (2006), *The Awakened One Poetics* (2010). *Sincerely Speaking Spiritually* (2020) and others. It's a great honor to have crossed paths with this worldwide award-winning poet and author. He always shares and spreads the Gospel's inspirational messages with humanity. He is a master of spirituality and humanity's daily uplifter, whom I consider not only my friend but my brother through Christ. Amen!

Dr. Katherine Stella
(Minnesota, USA)

This *International Family Poetry Anthology* is genuinely an inspirational revelation of God's precious grace. It's naturally a working miracle in this time and emerging era, especially with the negative impact of Covid-19 and its Delta and Omicron variants. Yet, it's uplifting, rejuvenating, and unites the spirit of love for family in fellowship and strengthening. Joseph, my dear cousin of excellence, whom I used to skip rope with, play jacks, and jump hopscotch on Baker Street and Clarence Lane in Jones Town, you have inspired our souls with your marvelous narration and God's words and works. Thank you, blessed cousin, for this dynamic family bond increasing book. May God's precious love and grace bless you always in all your endeavors.

Her Excellency, Dr. Noelene "Elaine" Christian
(United Kingdom)

Poetry is an excellent discourse where the writer expresses a variety of feelings. Today, the world suffers from the Covid-19 pandemic and the deadly virus that has shaken worldwide security and taken millions of lives. Reading this exceptional *International Family Poetry Anthology*, hosted by my dear brother, Professor, Ambassador, Dr. Joseph Spence Sr., brings us back to the bonds of family love and how that bond can provide encouragement and support. The bonding of love and togetherness articulated in each stanza of the poems are encouraging and convincing.

Dr. Kathirina Susanna Tati
(Malaysia)

DEDICATION

To my dearly beloved mother of God's inspirational grace, Dr. (h.c.) Mrs. Olive Maud Bainbridge-Spence, "Justice," and my dear father, Dr. (h.c.) Kenneth John Spence, "Moses," for all the beautiful things that each of you taught me. Additionally, to my brothers and sisters for all the beautiful times, we shared and will continue to share. To my extended family members, cousins, niece, nephews, and so on for your inspiration. Finally, dedication is extended to my children, grandchildren, Godchildren, and adopted children, who will always have my love and unique places in my heart. My sincerest thanks to each one of you. May God continue to shine His perpetual light upon you always from generation to generation.

To our ancestors on whose shoulders we have stood and garnished strength to continue our journey with words of ethics and integrity, uplifting our souls. Each of you has inspired and motivated heads to see a new light and day. Your roots have spread and grown among humanity worldwide. You have paved the way for us to live gracefully with humanity and experience God's gracious blessings.

In this Kwanzaa season, I say to each of you, "Ashe!" You have established God's divine light to guide our footsteps along the path; thus, allowing us to invoke righteousness and newfound inspiration in His grace for others to walk with love and reverence in His newfound light. Amen!

Have a fantastic day, continue to pray, stay encouraged, be healthy, live life lovingly, remain inspired, ingenious, resilient, motivated, uplifted, mindful, and enlightened with God's richest grace and blessings always!

CONTENTS

FORWARD

Family Strength Through Unity!

The literary essence of this uplifting *International Family Poetry Anthology* of inspirational grace is genuinely refreshing to the symmetry of the mind, body, and soul. It sends signs, symbols, signals, and English poetic conventions with a dynamic presence that transcends borders and continents with the harmonizing presence of God's grace.

This anthology is developed as a volume of transformative literary verses. Unfortunately, we could not have a family reunion because of Covid-19. As a result, we had to do something to bring the family together. I had just finished one Anthology on Covid-19. I was getting ready to write a serial edition to my tenth book of God's inspirational grace, "Sincerely Speaking Spiritually," with the title of "Get God's Grace." Suddenly, the thought came to me to write an *International Family Poetry Anthology.* Thus, this inspiring literary genre of noble poems showing appreciation and cherishing the family members was created.

This new paradigm of literary and poetic thinking enhances a new vision of correlation, thoughts, words, and deeds resulting in this enlightening anthology as a reality of God's love. Communications went to various family members; thus, gaining their support of submitting two poems, two articles, or a mixture of one poem and one article. The results were very inspiring. The impact of such is this persuasive anthology of poetic literary essence from God's harmonic grace.

The motivating decision to write about this unique theme came while conversing with family members. As a result, the list expanded. Selected subjects covered a broad spectrum of family events from childhood stories to family games, school nostalgic tales, visitations, and foods, covering every country where family members reside.

This decision is genuinely uplifting with an enriched theory of poetic narrative, sincerity, and positive episteme of understanding. The authors and poets proceeded on their precious path of ascending *Jacob's Ladder* with coordinated inspirational and dynamic verses.

The inspiring poem, *The Road Less Travelled*, by Robert Frost, sends an inspirational thought of, "Ways lead into ways and paths of inventiveness." Following this logical sequence, a motivating force led to this laudatory anthology from various angles; thus, it manifested itself and grew spontaneously based on the generated excitement.

Naturally, the essence of refreshing research was launched into operation to solidify this poetic literary process and undertaking. The dynamics opened many doors to non-biological poetic writers considered spiritual, sociological, psychological, anthropological, and physiological family members. This creative inclusion process launched a springboard developing the anthology; thus, reaching an exciting medium of poetic articulation and dynamic mixture of languages with inspirational prose and literary syntax.

Challenges encountered during the process appeared in various ways; however, the emotional resiliency from such was embraced, reflected, and converted into actionable accomplishments. Furthermore, such challenges were compellingly used as self-development tools to find worldwide family members; thus, enhancing the anthology's essence.

The main points and relevancy of this impressive anthology of literary, poetic, and impressive verses are motivating. One could perceive the essential thought reaching new heights obtained within the mind, body, and soul.

The relevancy of such intuitive and spontaneous actions generated the correct response leading to this astonishing poetic anthology. This book is the magnificent result of worldwide family members coming out and participating!

I sincerely applaud each of you for your creativity and eloquence, culminating in outstanding results from your cooperation, coordination, and collaboration in producing this anthology. Your actions resulted in this dynamic and action-packed anthology of soothing and thirst-quenching liquidity to uplift and stimulate the essence of our worldwide family members.

Your thoughts, words, deeds, communications, inspirations, and visualizations are positive. They resulted in natural, down-to-earth poetic language and expressions. Moreover, they revitalized the essential words to stimulate family members by implementing an objective correlation of English poetic literature to uplift and stimulate each others, mind, body, and soul, with this *International Family Poetic Anthology.*

May God's richest grace and blessing, which surpassed all understanding, rest, and abide with each one of you, your household, loved ones, and family members from generation to generation. Amen!

His Excellency, Ambassador, Professor,
Dr. Joseph S. Spence Sr.
Milwaukee, Wisconsin, USA
Epulaeryu Master!

PREFACE

The World's Dynamic Process — Poetry

Poetry is the dynamic and cosmic moving force of the mind, body, and soul. It makes a person whole and stimulates exploration of inspiration in the spirit to its very core. It invokes the process of creating, inspiring, and connecting life. It allows a person to become graciously entwined with and not tarnished with life. It teaches and brings an exceptional quality of mind, body, and soul connection into reality. It enables an internal and external blending to obtain a medium of equilibrium even if the pendulum swings in the opposite direction. In fact, poetic inspiration is God's words spoken in a different form and style for a gracious understanding and is a unique precious language of grace and reverence.

Poetic inspiration instills an orderly process of sanity. Additionally, it institutes a stabilization factor bringing to reality, out of contentiousness, a state of being that established order in a world spinning out of control. It's the more refined quality of existence. It enhances a precious and creative quality of life to obtain normality.

When applied to souls avoiding redemption, they refer to poetic inspiration as an elusive state of being since it does not exist in a vial or test tube, where it's capable of manipulation. It ascends the lack of order and brings tranquility where none existed before. It stimulates a revival of the spirit where such supposedly exists in a state of mundane dullness. It's an ongoing sensational revelation from God's prolific words bringing the mind, body, and soul in unity as a combined entity of graciousness.

Poetic inspiration enables an intertwining of the Blessed Trinity. It's an uplifting process where the rhapsody of the soul is touched deep within, causing the heart to resonate with new life. Poetic inspiration stimulates new life from God! It's spoken and unspoken words unto the senses, yearning for a higher order of creation. Where instability exists, it institutes God's stability through intercession and redemption.

Poetic inspiration is the unique revelation for a higher existence of the mind, body, and soul. Poetic inspiration is not static. It's a dynamic and moving force for souls to love one another, as God loves us (John 13:34). We must live in peace with our neighbors and let not our hearts be troubled (John 14:27), thus inspiring an uplifting of God's creation!

ACKNOWLEDGMENT

My dear and most precious family and friends, thanks to each one of you for allowing me to complete this *International Family Poetic Anthology*. Inspirations from each one of you rendered blessings during the journey. Indeed, words from each one of you were uplifting. I have learned a lot from you. The styles and forms of poetic writing covered will always stick with me in my growth as a poet and writer. They are very inspiring and educational, especially in learning how to use them with effectiveness, efficiency, and excellence.

My compliments to the various poetry sites where I am a member and participated in poetry writing and met many of you. My special thanks to them for bringing us together as a family and demonstrating our poetic articulation skills.

Many thanks to my friends for allowing me the time to participate in and complete this process. Indeed, you have missed my company and conversations. Realizing this was a precious cause, your approval without any disagreement sparked enlightenment.

My sincerest thanks to the editors of the following journals, anthologies, and magazines in which some of my poems, book reviews, and researched articles, not included in this manuscript, were previously published:

Achievers, University of Maryland, Adelphi, USA

Amaravati Poetic Prism, Andhra Pradesh, India

Atunis Poetry, Brussels, Belgium

Creative Launcher, Prayagraj, Uttar Pradesh, India

Cyberwit International Journal, Allahabad, India

Ewriter World, Nigeria, Africa

Ezine Articles, USA

Global Fusin Voices, Allahabad, India

Harvest of New Millennium, Allahabad, India

International Library of Poetry, MD, USA

International Who's Who in Poetry, MD, USA

Legion town Online, USA

MATC Times, Milwaukee, WI, USA

Parousia Magazine, Nigeria, Africa

Phoenix Magazine, Milwaukee Technical College, Milwaukee, Wisconsin, USA

Setu Bilingual Journal, Pennsylvania, USA

Shadow Porty Quarterly Magazine, MO, USA

Sound of Poetry Review, Athens, Greece

Sphinx Magazine, Baltimore MD, USA

Taj Mahal Review, Allahabad, India

The Edition Online, Bengali, India

The Ichabod, Washburn University, Topeka, Kansas, USA

Urban: Genre Creatives, Wisconsin, USA

Webster World, The Magazine of Webster University, MO, USA

World Haiku Association, Japan

World Poetry Alliance, United Kingdom

Thank you for your support and for helping me along the way. May God sincerely bless each one of you always!

Based on my declaration, every poet who submitted a poem is at this moment declared a co-author of this *International family Poetry Anthology!*

ENCOMIUM'S CULTURAL AND FAMILIAL VIRTUES!

Advancement changes natures' laws in many ways. While cultures, lifestyles, and etiquettes mingle and advance, there is an acute need for surveillance and vigilance to maintain a check and balance. Keep this in mind, the basic principles and family rules of bonding shouldn't be touched in any way.

This *International Family Poetry Anthology* of essence, upliftment, and love is apt and a well-deserved thought. Assimilating the family world's representatives is a superb effort with success. This accolade shows the purpose of the outpouring and poetic skills of our dear brother, Joseph.

Humanity from time immemorial has the essential, cultural, and practical virtues of an Encomium. It transcends from BC to AD. It uplifts and transforms old to new, dead to life, drought to harvest, and the oppressed to liberation. With the mercy of God, uplifting words, inspirational grace, and gracious and eloquent life-saving expressions, with genuine revival, it will last until eternity. If you want to uplift humanity, transformational forces are required, but people are unaware of its presence and fail to implement it properly.

This process may seem mysterious in some ways; however, an Encomium expresses love in spiritual words. Universal love can do everything since love is patient, love is kind and never envy. It's naturally simple, never boasts, and is never proud. Moreover, it does not dishonor anyone. It's not self-seeking, neither easily angered. Love crosses every barrier to prove and sustain itself. It keeps no record of "Wrongs" (1 Corinthians 13:4-8). The best spiritual force for humanity is to harmoniously uplift and illuminate the mind, body, and soul in equilibrium. Encomium moves, circulates, and stimulates deep into creations as an essential value of life. It's like the vital essence of enhancement in poetic, prose and literary narrations.

With delight, today, we pay respect to our dear brother, Joseph, for his literary talent. Since high school, his mother taught him how to write, read, recite, and interpret poetry. He has written various books and anthologies since with numerous poetic themes, and his actions have resulted in this *International Poetry Family Anthology*.

This family anthology is not the work of one day. Brother Joseph has continually spread love, peace, and humanity globally through his work, dedicated research, and implementation, which proved helpful in motivating and stimulating various literary personalities; thus, becoming his poetic family. The artistic curiosity of many is a medium for cognitive conventions with new challenges. Brother Joseph represents conscious ideas with this multidirectional and multicultural thematic, enhancing our family poetic fluidity.

The idea of an *International Family Poetic Anthology* (tough job) could not have come alive without the efforts of Brother Joseph. He knows how to adjoin family members to come forward with great inspiration. As a believer in God and humanity and a peace ambassador, Brother Joseph is very dear to all. He is a "Fauji" (army man) in a true sense, who never leaves any work undone and never leaves an effort. At this point in his age, he regularly finds quality time to take classes in literature and master himself to perform perfectly.

When asked why this topic? Brother Joseph states, "Family unity is the base of love and togetherness. It brings peace and harmony. It's the best way to work collectively for an anthology, exchanging each other's thoughts, and maintaining inspirational peace in the family."

Nothing comes easy in life without challenges, and for him, "Finding family members worldwide was the most challenging." However, peace, love, and harmony enhanced closeness amongst all of us. It generates happiness and faith for rejoicing as we create betterment for all.

My heartfelt applaud, dear Brother Joseph for this tribute of joyful expressions, love, and dedication for this note-worthy *International Family Poetry Anthology*. This anthology will enlighten family members with creativity, motivation, inspiration, and the proliferation of togetherness for years to come.

This graceful *International Family Poetic Anthology* results from cooperation, coordination, and collaboration with the worldwide family. It's a springing well of soothing and thirst-quenching water of vibrant poetic verses that are stimulating, uplifting, and enhancing the unity of the mind, body, and soul.

My most gracious Brother Joseph, your visualization of positive poetic literature portrays the proper symmetry of thoughts, words, deeds, and essential stimulation. Your artistic curiosity is a medium of creative motivation, chronological expression, and English cognitive conventions. Your descriptive English lexicon narrates excellent expression and representation with a multidirectional, multi geographical, multilinguistic, and multicultural thematic fluidity in a new light and uplifts the family's essence.

May God's grace, surpassing all understanding, abide with the entire family. Let it be a combined and successful operational team. Let it touch all loved ones and household members, from generation to generation, in all undertakings.

I proudly applaud you for your gracious efforts. You're most trustworthy and a role model. I pray for your success in this project, destiny, family, blessings, and God's wishes to all.

Dr. Manjula Asthana Mahanti
Retired Educator (India).

Dr. Olive M "Justice" Bainbridge-Spence (h.c.)

This picture represents my dearly beloved mother of God's inspirational grace, Dr. (h.c.) Olive M.Bainbridge Spence. Many called her "Justice." She received this name from community members because she always helped others with their legal and marital issues. People came from near and far to see her and resolve their issues. She is the revered "Justice of the Peace!"

I truly miss walking with my mother in the early morning breeze before going to school. We walked and talked about God. Justice was my most favorite and closest friend.

She taught me how to read, interpret, write, and recite poetry in high school. Now, I write in her honor to uplift her legacy, memory, persona, and aura in God's grace!

She was the best cook in town. People used to come by and get a plate of food from her. I genuinely appreciate those days and the delicious meals she cooked for us.

Justice, I love you very dearly, and we shall meet one day again in the future in God's glorious kingdom and sing the sweet songs of grace you taught me!

Justice, these are your accolades
Blessings Great Mom!

Justice, you will always remain foremost in my heart as my dearly beloved and precious mother of God's inspirational grace! God's riches, grace, and blessings to you always!

Dr. Kenneth John "Moses" Spence (h.c.)

This picture represents my dear father, Dr. (h.c.) Kenneth John "Moses" Spence. Many called him "Moses" because he always helped others out of bondage, like Moses, who helped the children of Israel out of bondage to freedom from Pharaoh through the Reds Sea. Some also called him "Red Shirt." He received the name from many who said he had a bleeding heart for helping others. They could see the blood from his heart spreading over his shirt; therefore, they called him "Red Shirt!"

Moses took us swimming every month. He was a great swimmer. I genuinely appreciate those days and the swimming lessons received. In addition, I find great pleasure in telling people how I learned to swim. They often asked, "Your dad took you swimming and taught you how to swim. Where are you from?" It's incredible. I could not believe the response or even why there was a question of that nature. I was expecting a response such as, "Man, that's so awesome!"

Moses, these are your accolades!
Blessings Great Dad!

Moses, my beloved and blessed father, thanks for all the great times we spent together and enjoyed. I loved riding with you on the donkey cart. That was great. I loved your idea of how to drive on a one-way street. When I asked you how? You responded,

"Just back up all the way." I recalled laughing as you were doing the same. I love the punch you made with Guinness Stout, milk, vanilla, nutmeg, and eggs at Christmas for the family with lovely Hanna Town Bakery Spiced Buns.

Blessings to you always. One day we will see each other again in God's glorious kingdom. You have always spoken about the land of milk and honey. That's it. We will be able to have a delicious drink of milk and honey when we meet again!

FIRST CERTIFICATES ISSUED!

The First Certificate issued went to my dearly beloved sister, Marsha Spence, Florida, U.S.A. The call for submissions went out on December 23, 2020, and her submission was received on December 28, 2020, as the first one. Each person who submitted their first poem also received a certificate of the same magnitude as a poet.

SECOND CERTIFICATES ISSUED!

*T**he Second Certificate*** was awarded to the first person who submitted their first two poems. The award went to my dearly beloved cousin, Dr. Sandra Y. Spence, schoolteacher, Montego Bay, Jamaica. On January 2, 2021, her two poems were received ten days after the submission request was sent. Each person who submitted their two poems also received a certificate of the same magnitude with my signature as the advisor to the World Parliament for Peace, India!

POETIC SUBMISSIONS!

Poetic inspiration comes from all angles, day and night. When or how poetic proliferation is penned has many permutations like a grain of sands in the Sahara Desert. It comes anytime from anywhere and in any situation of life. It could be sealed in a bottle cast onto the oceans' tides for future generations to discover. It could be derived from a Peniel Experience with God or in the moment of experiencing bewilderment of existential joy gracing the mind, body, and soul with much inspiration.

My beloved baby sister of God's inspirational grace, Marsha, scribed the following poem on Sunday, December 27, 2020. She sent it at 12:51 pm. I opened it at 8:27 am the next day. It came days before the anthology's kick-off date. The request was sent to her on December 23, at 2:30 am. She rose to the call of duty and diligently acted above and beyond expectations. It is the first poem to grace the *"International Family Poetic Anthology."*

Marsha states, "Joe, I went for a walk and spent an hour working out at the gym. After that, I returned home, got comfortable, and then penned this acrostic poem entitled:

"OH, MY BROTHERS!"

Oh, my brothers!

How many brothers?

Many are my brothers

Younger and older are my brothers

Bad and Good are my brothers

Remembering all my brothers

Oh, my brothers

Teachers to me are my brothers

Heaven help my brothers

Every day, I think of my brothers

Remembering all my brothers

Savior, have mercy on my brothers!

Dr. Marsha P. Spence (Florida)

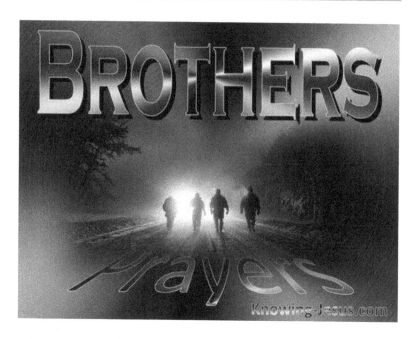

My sister and I have been close since childhood. We cherished the biblical connection of *Mary* and *Joseph*. I spent more time with her than any of my siblings. She is very optimistic, a great vegetarian cook, and makes nutritious natural juices. Whenever I used to visit her, we would always attend church and take my dear mother new flowers at her earthly resting site in Florida. We went biking, walking, and played great games of ping pong, and she loved my poetry books. We have always been supportive of each other. She is and always will be a dear soul and blessed sister unto eternity through God's grace and everlasting blessings on her soul!

The Second Poem to grace and kick off this *International Family Poetic Anthology* is for my big-up cuz, Father T. Mosley. He is my mother's sister, Aunt Tuncy's son, and is the best radio DJ in the UK, who hosts the Soup & Dumpling Show of TGM Radio, UK!

FATHER T. MOSLEY—SWEET SOUP & DUMPLING LINGUIST!

Tony Father T Mosley, my cuz of great and inspiring dignity.

I love the music he spins, rightly rocking humanity.

TGM Radio, what a great show, everyone should know.

Tony Father T Mosley, spinning reggae, what a great show!

My big-up cuz to heart. That's the way it was from the start.

Breda man with a musical plan, jamming across the land.

Soup and dumpling show. This kina food mek you grow

Sprinkle some Pikapeppa Sauce flava ina it and sip it slow.

With Her Majesty's military, cuz faithfully served England.

Saluted and sung the anthem, "God save our gracious queen."

The best DJ ina di UK plays music to spin. Music is mean!

Listening to TMG Radio, di rockas make you lick a pipe!

Empress kiss him every day. She keeps her man on his plan.

Tony Father T, spins reggae, you know, what a great show!

Em luv ackee, saltfish, mackerel, and banana wid Red Strip.

Cuz, big-up wid rockas, touching humanity wid a nice flow.

Soup and dumpling show. This kina food mek you grow

My linguistical cuz, rap Potwa, Patois, Rasta, British English.

He is up and down wid it. Roots knowledge he knows

Distinguished, not extinguished, Father T. Mosley, Linguist!

Dr. Joseph S. Spence Sr. (Wisconsin)

(Jamaican Soup and Dumpling Dish)

The Third Poem addresses existentialism. Many have found that the theory of enlightenment and existentialism are inspirational and uplifting. Additionally, Abraham Maslow's Theory of Motivation is natural, functional, calls for coordination, collaboration, teamwork, and is a holistic quality of life with all three combined!

WHO AM I ? ? ?

Who am I really?

Where am I really?

Why am I even here?

What is all "this" about anyway?

When will I ever know?

How will I ever know?

Questions abound

Answers, Anyone?

My family of God's grace!

Dr. Carla F. Spence, ESQ *(S. Korea)*

LOOKING OUT TODAY— THE WINDOW OF LIVE (VISUALIZATION)

As I looked out today, I see:
Family members move diligently, with the purpose of God ordering their steps. Some smiling, rushing, walking, crawling, but all pressing onward.

As state in Philippians 3:14, "I press toward the mark for the prize of the high calling of God in Christ Jesus."

As I looked out today, I see:
Blue sky, birds flying, chirping, sipping nectar from flowers. Trains moving, planes flying, rain from clouds, and a rainbow forming.

As stated in Revelation 4:3, "And he that sat was to look upon like a jasper and a sardine stone: and there was a rainbow round about the throne, with a sight like unto an emerald."

Looking out today, I see:
Concrete highways, cars busily driving, bikes riding, skateboards zooming. Life moves along happily, not sadly, showing God's inspired grace.

As stated in Ephesians 2:8, "For by grace are ye saved through faith; and not of yourselves: it is the gift of God."

Looking out today, I see:

Mended fences, beautiful gardens growing, God's inspired family members smiling. Sad people are not crying, seeking a new way, a new day, and new light.

As stated in Corinthians 4:16, "For which cause we faint not. But though our outward man perishes, yet the inward man is renewed day by day."

As I looked today, I can see:
Growth opportunities, roses blooming, nice fragrance smelling. New possibilities of life beaming, darkness erased by God's light.

As stated in Ephesians 5:8, "For ye were sometimes darkness, but now are ye light in the Lord: walk as children of light."

As I look out today, I see my family:
A new horizon generating from the red evening sunset. Uplifting a nation in unity with God's love, prosperity, and blessings. Enhancing one's quality of life to reach high— like a shining star!

As stated in Revelation 22:16, "I Jesus have sent mine angel, to testify unto you these things in the churches. I am the root and the offspring of David and the bright and morning star."

Dr. Joseph S. Spence Sr. (Wisconsin)

MOTHER

A

Mother

So divine.

Children she loves.

Angels brightly smile on her from above!

MOTHER'S ACROSTIC

Mothers are indeed God's gift to the world and really for us.

Oh, they will put things out, even a fuss, with a simple touch.

The essence of their being prevents us from being in a rush.

Hear their words of wisdom, and one will learn very much.

Even as drivers, they shift gears without scraping the clutch.

Resting a child's head, they simmer a cry with such a hush.

Saving grace, loving us dearly, like a hand with a royal flush!

Dr. Joseph S. Spence, Sr *(Wisconsin)*

(Mothers are God's precious gifts to humanity)

MI MADA STIMULATING SOUP AND DUMPLING!

Ital Soup and Dumpling

Mi mada used to cook it.

Mek me lick mi finga.

Mi want more from the Dutch pot

Me mada used to say, "Bwoy mind it bine you!"

Mek it wid cornmeal or flowa

Mi breda, it good any hour

Dem dumpling tight

Mada always says, "Dumpling must have on a jacket!"

Cook it wid a few okuroo.

Yellow yam

Gungo peas

Piece of chopping down chow

Likkle scotch bonnet.

Sprinkle some black peppa.

Slice up an onion.

Keep you finga from your eye.

Better don't forget the pumpkin

And a couple of green bananas.

Mek it simma dung

Blend wid some pic-a-peppa sauce

Likkle salt to taste

Soup ago sweet Mon!

Call everybody.

Mek dem sidung

Pass the duchie pan the right-hand side

Serv out a good helping deh

"Mek me loosen up mi belt!"

Dr. Father Tony Mosley *(United Kingdom)*

FAMILY RAKSHA BANDHAN

Striking cords displayed around

in the marketplace, glittering and lively.

The ambiance is gloriously bright.

Groups of girls, in their best attire

watchful everywhere,

selecting threads of their choice.

These vivid strings look simple

but have great importance—symbolically!

They are named— "Rakhi"—sacred threads!

On the auspicious day of "Raksha Bandhan."

A very pious and meaningful festival,

sisters tie "Rakhi," Raksha Sutra

on the wrist of brothers after praying and painting

"Tika" on the foreheads of their brothers.

This act indicates love and faith in their brothers

that they will protect them from every evil.

Brothers "Credent" about their sister's loving care.

The bonding of persuasion, oneness, duties amongst siblings

become more strong—sustainable!

Brothers gift sisters as a token of affection

joyous moments furbishing the whole family.

Keep the melody of their relationship—"Sweet and fresh!"

Dr. Manjula Asthana Mahanti *(India)*

(Rakhi being tie around the wrist of a brother by his sister)

GOD'S FAMILY ANGELIC SEVEN SEPTET SERIES

His Words

through His mighty words

power manifestation

when you obey Him

His Faith

faith is evidence

inner substance of the soul

God fulfilling needs

Open Doors

God will open doors

always shut by humankind

He will make a way

Revelation

the day is coming

truth shall be revealed on earth

evil shall not win

His Angels

the spirit of God

angels standing by His saints

love insulation

Repentance

trusting in His words

repentance of mortal souls

it is time to pray

His Baptism

God will bless His saints

as they walk through the fire

with His baptism

DEDICATED TO MY MOM: MRS. EUGENIE SPENCE

The Greatest Elocutionist Ever

They all sat earnestly

Waiting to hear you deliver

Heaven's Grocery Store in refined style

No one mumble

Because they knew that the encore

could mean Grumble

Or who knows which one would come

from your great repertoire

Your diction and expression were well thought out.

My dedicated mother uplifting God's love

You were indeed an excellent Elocutionist!

Dr. Sandra Y. Spence *(Jamaica)*

MISSING YOU—"KEKE!"

You stole my heart
And became my heartbeat
You gave me the sweetest hugs
And kisses ever.

You make me feel like a real mummy
I feel as though I gave birth to you.

I asked myself daily
When will I get those warm hugs and kisses again?
I loved you then
I love you now
I will love you forever!

Author's Notes: This poem is dedicated to my grand-niece,
Keyuanna "Keke" Barrett.

Dr. Sandra Y. Spence (Jamaica)

(Pearly Gates of Heaven)

ME JAMAICAN DISH—ACKEE & SALT FISH!

Aww, me Ackee and Saltfish

How I can't do without you

You're my number one Jamaican dish

When I fix you up with seasoning

You pass humankind for reasoning

When I fix you up with salt and pepper

All the family comes ready to eat!

Leave the English with them Fish and Chips

Me satisfied with I Ackee and Saltfish!

Her Excellency, Dr. Noelene Christian (United Kingdom)

(Jamaican Ackee and Saltfish Dish with Dumplings)

FAMILY COMES FIRST!

Stepped in after a long exile

Decked up with a sorrowful smile is the old Banyan tree

A great pillar of memorable civilization and culture

Incredible symbol of kindness, affection, and morality

Like our old grandparents, imparting the values

A witness to the family's past grandeur

Welcomed at the door with innumerable memories

Replica of our family's traditions

Love, care, concern for everyone displayed a prime tender

Providing shelter to everyone when in distress

All stand and joined hands if any mess

Festival or celebrations, no festivity without all members

Togetherness, a significant idiosyncrasy of our family

Family is a porch to the world and a prime school of values

We are civilized. We, 'coz our elders nurtured us

This was life in our homes, now barren house only

All loving members are now in an eternal abode.

Alone and unguarded, our blessings and concerns are lost

Keep a strong bonding as the family comes first

Our identity is the reason for our joy and smiles

Be a solid rock for the foundation

Of Your Family!

Dr. Manjula Asthana Mahanti (India)

(Family members deserves our best of God's grace and blessings)

LIVING THE DREAM?

Living the Dream

What does that even mean?

Traveling the world

Always being seen.

Do you know the "Dream of You?"

Do you know—really know—

Who to be?

I want to know—really—

The dream of me.

So, I'm seeking

What about you?

Are you seeking?

The dream of you?

Dear family, please enlighten me!

Dr. Carla F. Spence, Esq. *(South Korea)*

(Dreams take us beyond into a new dimension)

IT'S A FAMILY NEW DAY!

Why are you so sad and lonely?

Look, it's a new day!

The birds are singing.

My family members are blooming.

The butterflies are doing what Mother Nature has taught them
to do.

Look at the lights begging for you to embrace them

Do you know why?

No, you don't!

The master has come, and He is calling you.

So, break every shackle that binds you,

And embrace the sunlight that awaits you.

Open your windows and doors -

"A new day. A New light awaits you!"

You are free because you're resistant and resilient.

So, let your freedom resonate far and wide.

"It's a new day!"

Dr. Barbara Antonie *(Maryland, USA)*

(Christ resurrection certainly is a new beginning)

HOW RICH WE WERE!

We came from this little town in Kingston, called Jones Town. My father was a barber, well known, because of his humor and his kindness. When people come from the country looking for their loved ones, they end up at 37 Baker Street, asking questions using the last known address.

My loving father, who always had a jug of lemonade or sugar and water, would go across the street, get some fried fish and bread, feed them, then lock up the shop and start on the hunt for the family members they could not find or hear from in years.

My father had the only barbershop not just in the neighborhood but in the entire town. People came to have their hair cut and trimmed from all over. The barbershop was a place for great conversation and laughter while others waited for their turn to get a haircut. Joviality permeated the place with much grace.

The fellows congregate outside the barbershop on the weekends, awaiting the man selling roast peanut on his bike and the other one selling boiled, seasoned, and tasty shrimps. They had great conversations while there. Some of the fellows called my father "Lobster." That was a nickname they gave him, which they enjoyed during their conversations.

My father found most of the missing people. I never stopped loving him. When he died, Christmas day 1962, my world was shattered. He was a simple man who lived a life helping others and loved his family.

Dr. Barbara Antonie (Maryland, USA)

(Abundance is having so much without the realization)

THE ATTITUDE OF GRATITUDE

Life is a continuous family journey
Sometimes you feel left alone
And others left behind

On the pathway to blessings
I did meet the attractive gratitude as a companion
Who told me, "Blessings, tiny or great deserve *thanks*."

Family life is a blessing
You are living
Not non-living
Isn't this worth "The thanks" on your knees?!

With gifted hands on the family table of togetherness
Sharing the meal of love and oneness
Isn't this grace worth gracing the day with "Thanks?"

If thou not appreciate gratitude
Then more blessings will give an attitude
Of great feeling welcomed by you

Thanksgiving is a light of pulchritude
Beam it, and thou shall see the beauty of benison
The hidden being of gratitude becomes an open blessing

Don't tighten the lips of your heart
Let the family thanks smile from ear to ear
Think thanks, give gratitude to "The ALMIGHTY!"
Who gave you the gift of family
Even the gift of this moment that the dead pray and wish they
had!

Ambassador Dr. Lovelyn P Eyo (Nigeria, Africa)

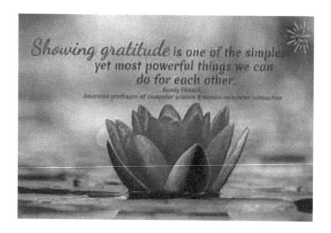

GRANDMA'S OLIVE WORDS (ACROSTIC POEM)!

Often, I think of the things that grandma told me in her

Loving arms. The way she'd hold me.

I'd complain of a new married fight.
She'd say, "Don't worry, child, things will be alright." Her

Very wise words dancing in my

Ear. "One has to be the water,
While the other one is on fire." Subtly suggesting how to maintain our love and desire.
Grandma's words have continued to grow deep within me.
"Gone but never forgotten!"

Dr. Sonni Ramirez (Maryland, USA)

(We will never forget Grandma Olive)

MY MOTHER'S HATS

My mother was a woman of many hats
Literally and metaphorically.
Her broad-rimmed black hat covered her from the sun
And reminds her of dutiful care for everyone.

Her white hat was for church
This temple was the place she worked.
And a reminder of her truths
Her dedication to this her very roots.

She had a variety of coloured straw hats
To match any blouse, shoe, and frock.
This elegance spoke of her coordination
And the flair she had for fashions.

A covered head shows nobility
Each hat fits into the social hierarchy.
It's no wonder then she made sure
She had a hat for every cure.

My mother was a fashionista

With a hat completing each attire.

Symbols of authority and power

Were the hats of my "Dear Mother!"

Dr. Paulette Spence-Hines *(Jamaica, West Indies)*

(Such fanciful and graceful hats)

AN ANGELIC FAMILY FROM THE INFINITE SKY

It was a sunny day, and an angel came before my eyes

I was unhappy, thinking about those who are blind.

She asked me, "Why don't your efforts rise?"

There is an Angelic Family with a shining prize

She was courageous, made me a man of humankind.

The way that angel says

From her lovely coral lips.

Removed darkness from my way

My mystical soul was amazed when I felt an eternal kiss.

She was sunlight in my day, lighting my way.

The hidden corners of my heart became illuminated.

My family came from everywhere with inspiration.

She said, "Never shut the doors of your senses at night and in the day."

That adorable angel made my life delighted.

An Angelic Family from the Infinite Sky!

Ambassador, Dr. Ashok Kumar Verma (India)

(Angels are everywhere waiting to assist us)

FAMILY UNITY (ACROSTIC POEM)

Family Structure

Allowing God's Good Grace

Merits And Standards

Into Hearts Homes And

Lengths Darken Plights too

Yet Still Prays for

"United We Stand!"

Not Divided We Fall

In This I Ask

Through Power Of Christ

Yesterday, Today, And Tomorrow

(Amen)

Dr. Katherine Stella (Wisconsin, USA)

(Family are one in God's precious name)

TOMBOY: MONORHYME POEM!

Born in the summer of '59.

I was, *"The 9 of 10 Divine!"*

German and Italian like fine wine.

Five boys and five girls

Mom could not keep the floors shining.

Dad trimmed trees.

Mom wrestling boxes with grind

But making sure our *"Lord's Table!"*

She always had an exceptional shine.

Snow up to our knees and walking blind.

School's hills were not my kind.

Hooky bobbing in straight lines.

Cave adventures, corn fritters, vanilla wafers, bologna sandwiches,

all the freaking time.

Now, this mom has a mini-me and

that is just fine.

50 years have passed, and I

still think and reflect on

past friends of mine.

Hoping, praying, they're all

doing well and truly fine!

(Amen)

Dr. Katherine Stella (Wisconsin, USA)

Notes: My great United States Army sister, Kathy, and I have been friends for over twenty years. We both crawled through mud, drank black coffee at 2: 00 am when it's freezing in the foxhole downrange when the first sergeant comes with his coffee pot. It tasted like turpentine! We both know about "Hurry Up and Wait." This one takes the cake, "No matter what. Don't drop your M16 Rifle." You will have to "Get Down With It." Start pushing away at Mother Earth to build up your muscles. We made our "Marksmanship Qualifications" on the shooting range when it's cold. We know all the cadence songs. They kept us moving. The GI Parties on the weekends were very entertaining. She is a down-to-earth and a "Real Sista" who operates where the rubber meets the road. Thanks to Uncle Sugar, we are full of gusts and vinegar!

JAMAKA FAMILI STILE MAKREL RUNDUNG WID COCONAT MILK!

Use fres coconat milk, tomatoe, onyion, scotch bonnet peppa,
and red bell peppa

Caanmeal dumplin, couple peg a bredfrut, two slice a yella yam,
or

White yam, Renta yam, St. Vincent yam, or Afu yam.

Don't figet a cuple finga a green banana, Maann, mek di dinna
yummy yum!

Mek mi tell yu how fi put dis togeda.

Boil out di salt from outa di mackerel, and res it pon di side fi
likkle a wile!

Den, put on yu coconat milk pan the fiya, and bile it dung to
custad till it pop ile

Den, cut up yu onyion, tomatoe, scotch bonnet peppa, red bell
peppa, and put it ina de ile.

Stir yu pot till de seasoning cook, den add yu whyte cane vinega
fi bring up de flava.

Put in de mackerel dem, cova dung de pot, wid de pot cova

Tun dung de stove, and mek it simma dung fi a likkle wile!

Den, tek yu pot off a de fiya,

With yu caanmeal dumplin, yu green banana, two slices of yella yam, or

St. Vincent yam, Afu yam, White yam, and a cuple peg a bredfruit,

And if you have wonn sweet potato, add it to di pile.

Put on de pot cova pon de pot, and mek e beil!

Put yu serving dish dem pon di table.

Put yu rundung, wid yu mackerel, cut ina small peces.

Sprinkle wid a likkle blak peppa pon di tap ina one a de servin dish.

Den, put yu yam, caanmeal dumplin, green banana, wid di bredfruit, ina di nada dish

Cut up a grenn avocado pear, some sweet fried plantin, an serve dem pon de side

Everyone tek dem seat a de table in front a dem dina plate and don't be late,

Cum ya famili dinna is now served!

Clasp yu han, close yu ey, an tank God, fi de food.

Dis ya di devotion fi de portion

Tek yu caanmeal dumplin, groun provision and put it pon yu dinna plate

Den yu mackerel, custad an ile pon de top.

Laaaard, man, dis yaa dina yaa, a finga likinnng gooood!

(Written in Patwaa)

Dr. S. B. Spence (New York)

JAMAICAN FAMILY STYLE MACKEREL RUNDUNG WITH COCONUT MILK!

Always use fresh coconut milk, tomato, onion, scotch bonnet pepper, and red bell pepper. That's the best way. Also, include some cornmeal dumplings, a couple pegs of green breadfruit, two slices of yellow yam or white yam, renta yam, saint vincent yam, or afu yam. Also, don't forget to add a couple fingers of green banana. This diverse ingredient makes your dinner very yummy!

When all the ingredients are ready, put this all together in a unique way. First, boil out the salt from the mackerel, and rest it off to the side for a couple of minutes. After that, put the coconut milk on the fire, and let it boil down until you see the custard on the oil. After that, slice up the onions, tomatoes, scotch bonnet peppers, red bell peppers, and place them in the oil.

Continue stirring the pot of ingredients until the seasonings are correctly glazed. Then add some white vinegar to enhance the flavoring. At this point, place the mackerels in the pot, and place the cover on the pot. Turn down the stove and let everything simmer down for a little while.

After simmering down:

Stir with the cornmeal dumplings, green bananas, slices of yellow yams selected, and green breadfruit pegs.

If you have any sweet potatoes, add one or two in the pot also.

Place the cover back on the pot and let it boil for a few minutes. Listen, my family. When this is completed, place your serving dishes on the table. Cut the mackerel into small pieces in a separate dish. Sprinkle a dash of black pepper on top of the mackerel. Then place the yam, cornmeal dumplings, green bananas, and the breadfruit pegs in a separate dish. Finally, slice up a nice avocado (pear), some fried plantains, and serve that as a treat on the side.

Everyone should take their seats as a family at the table by their dinner plates. They should not be late because dinner is ready and it's time to serve. Don't forget to clasp your palms, close your eyes, and render thanks and praise to God for the delicious meal as your devotion for your portion. Finally, take a cornmeal dumpling and other provisions, and place them on your dinner plate. Then place the mackerel, custard, and oil on the top.

My family says, "Yes, Lord, this dinner is genuinely finger-licking good!"

Dr. S. B. Spence *(New York)*

(Mackrel Coconut Style Rundung)

I'M AFRAID!

God,

I'm terrified

the air around me

the grass I tread on

are seeded by the virus

that destroys family happiness.

God,

In my prayers, I glorify You

So that You will touch restless hearts and confused minds

So they will break this chain of darkness

Bestow sustenance on those whose

Livelihoods are impeded for their families

Heal those who are fighting for their lives

Bless those who try to save them

Bless the noble people

Enlighten the minds of our leaders

Give success to our researchers

So they will defeat this virus

Only to You we surrender

God, save Your creations.

God, I fear

For the wrong step taken

Would You please protect my dear family?

For demons are rampant.

Dr. Kathirina S. Tati *(Malaysia)*

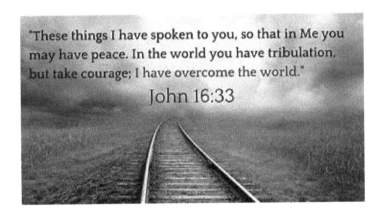

"These things I have spoken to you, so that in Me you may have peace. In the world you have tribulation, but take courage; I have overcome the world."

John 16:33

MOTHER'S CRY

Oh God,

Today we are so along at home.

Our food is mere rice with boiled vegetables

Fortunately, the soil is still fertile

Occasional rains come to help water

For our sustenance, we are grateful

Although the child asks, "Where are the delicacies?"

My heart bleeds to answer!

I am not alone

Trying to wipe away tears

Worried that the children are sad

They do not yet know the meaning of suffering.

God,

When will Covid-19 be defeated?

When will this pandemic end?

Why are things stagnant?

Please allow the sales of village vegetables and food.

Allow the exchange of money

And bring food to my table.

We desperately wait for Covid-19 erasure.

Our savings are empty.

I have crystal clear water for my baby

But she craves milk, and her whimpers cut into my soul.

God,

My husband can only cry sitting in a wheelchair

His moan begging for forgiveness from me

For not being able to lighten my load.

God, my voice cries out to You!

Dr. Kathirina S. Tati *(Malaysia)*

DESTRUCTION

This year begins with grief

All over the world. Humans collapsed because of this disease

Here and there, moaning groans into nothingness.

I mourn and give alms.

My family also needs Your "Balm of Gilead!"

Without realizing it, my country was invaded.

Oh my God, my country is not as advanced as other countries

Developed and high-tech countries.

Who knows death without a weapon?

Against this strange virus

Supposedly human-made weapons

To fight for power, for victory.

God, I believe You will let us out for a moment.

You will close Your eyes temporarily.

Your creation will repent.

Ego and greed do not want You

When You created the heavens and the earth.

This plague is the result of egotism and greed.

As we had forgotten Your law

When You created the earth and its contents

But my Lord, I believe in Your promise.

When there are two or more

Glorifying You in prayers asking for forgiveness.

You will listen to us. My family prays!

My God, please end the Covid-19 pandemic.

That is destroying your creation.

Amen!

Dr. Kathirina S. Tati *(Malaysia)*

BIO TERRORISM—NO FUN!

Can our family's sweet, soft souls bear them?

How selfish and inhumane they're.

Let's do what we can

Is destruction so far?

Oh! Humble hearts are afraid

Will the green nature be red?

How can our eyes forget the pandemic?

Why don't we think about civic?

Oh! The beautiful world can't bear them.

Family, be united, save humanity, let's do what we can.

Humbleness, truth, and values are our concerns

Changes in nature aren't any fun

They have viruses, and they have a dangerous gun.

Will our weak lungs bear diseases?

Why do they want war?

Is the world ready for it so far?

They always give our souls red scar

My family, can we imagine our future?

Almighty God, save our planet, all creatures, and our family!

***Ambassador, Dr. Ashok Kumar Verma** (India)*

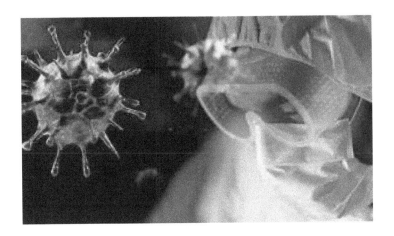

LIZAD INA DE GUAVA TRE!

De dey a luvly yukno breda. Sun a shyne out

Mi couch mesef in a de guava tre

Sedung pon a solid lim

Mi a chil wid som ital breez

Mi drif ina a daydremin fe a spel

Masa, wen mi opun up mi ey.

Mi seee dis ya likkle lizad a stare ina mi face.

Den im stick out im tung, an mi jump

Scare to ded, yu no?

Mi glad im was a polly lizad

If im was one a dem crooken lizad mi wouda ded!

Mi neva sa one wod, couldn't even screm

Mi jus ganee, dred mi disaper

Mi jump out a de guava tre

Lan pan mi fot.

Nex ting mi kno, mi clohs ter off ina de tre

Mi frock huk up pon a lim

De tred wha sew de gaterin cum out

Mi hav one likkle inch lef rap roun mi waise

De polly lizad scare mi out a de guava tre

Man, mi jump out a de tre but mi

Skirt a hokup pon a lim wen mi jump out de tre

De botam path a mi cloth goneee—skirt missin.

Mi mada se mi an startee laufin

Shee knoo wha hapin wid de lizad ina de guava tre

Mama staaat fi tel de peple dem bout wha hapen

De peple a lok cros dem fence pan mi

Mi run ome an lef mama wen she staaat telin de peple dem

Afta mi rech ome, mi change mi cloth

Mi go ina de back yadde an plaa

Chilin an a simma dung

Grani se mi a staat bus out a laughin to

Dat a de legenn of mi lifee

Mi usee to luve lisen to grani repeat de 27th Psalm

She repeat it dat day fe mi

She usee to cal mi cussshu puss!

Her Excellency, Dr. Noelene Christian (United Kingdom)

GREEN POLLY LIZARD IN THE GUAVA TREE!

It was a lovely and sunny day outside. I took a seat in a low-growth guava tree to relax. Sitting on a solid limb, I felt relaxed. The breeze was very calm and rustled through the leaves. It was so refreshing. I started daydreaming slightly. There was a big surprise when I opened my eyes.

Lord! A green lizard, was sitting there. It was very bold and stared right into my face. Next, he stuck out his tongue at me. I was scared to death and jumped out of the tree. I am so glad it was only a green Polly Lizard. If it were a giant croaking lizard, I probably would be dead. Those monsters are ugly and crazy.

I never said one word. I couldn't even scream. It was time for me to disappear. I just jumped from the tree with a leap of faith. Thank God, I landed on both feet, standing.

The next thing I knew, my skirt was caught in the tree. It was caught on a branch when I jumped.

And all the sewn gathering immediately came out. All I had left around me was about an inch around my waist. The Polly lizard scared the life out of me. Now, my skirt is hookup on a branch in the Guava Tree. The lizard can have it. I am not going back to get it.

The bottom part of my clothing was gone—skirt missing. My mother saw me and started laughing. She knew what happened with the lizard in the guava tree. Mama told all the people the story. They laughed also. People were looking over their fence at me. I ran home and left my mother telling the story.

After getting home, I changed clothing. Then, I went into the backyard and started playing. It was relaxing, and I began to simmer down. My granny saw me. She also heard the story and was laughing. That was the legend of my life. I loved to listen to my granny reciting the 27th Psalm.

She recited it that day for me, and I felt better. She used to call me "Chusshu Puss!"

Her Excellency, Dr. Noelene Christian *(United Kingdom)*

MY SWEET SIXTEEN

My dear mother, in two thousand and six
Your silence went on a journey
Leaving me with words-
A gift, a treasure
"Go with God, and you will be okay."
These words I take up and down the lane

My dear mother, when all seems odd
On those words, I give a nod
A lost voice
My heart lost its poise
As the night lays
And the day delays
When will you return!
The time shrugs left forlorn.

Anthonia, my sweet sixteen
With your prayers, I am blessed to win
This known on earth
Yes, Angels hide their wings
Within the rhythm of hearts
I can hear you sing
Riding on the wings of my heart
Humming in your new home
Sweet songs of hope!

Blessings always, my dear mother!

Ambassador, Dr. Lovelyn P. Eyo (*Nigeria, Africa*)

(Cheers, Big Dad. Do have a blessed day!)

EPULAERYU

Universal unity

Taste buds on fire

There is always room for more

Mom needs bigger pots

Placing Heavens call

Please respond

Yes!

Dr. Katherine Stella (*Wisconsin, USA*)

GREAT CHILDHOOD COUSINS ROCK!

Joseph, Beverley, and I (Elaine)

Up and down Clarence Lane

We were like three peas in a pod

Couldn't be separated by anyone

We skipped rope, played jacks, and jumped hopscotch.

We used to climb the Guinepe tree

And them so delicious and so sweet

Then the Coolie Plums

They tasted so lovely and sweet

You would think they were dipped in honey.

Well, Hairy Mangoes were my favourite fruits

Of all yummy and yum, I think they were called (common mango)

The only trouble is that after you eat them you have to

Find a pin to remove the hairs from between your teeth

Some people used their fingers.

At my Aunt Olive's shop, it was great

The line was always long with people

They wanted their fried salt fish and dumplings

She sold cooked food and raw food

Also, banana, yam, dashine, and natural stuff

The people constantly came and showed their precious love!

That's the way I saw it, and remember the precious doves

The blended ingredients pigeon soup was delicious!

Don't give away the powerhouse secret; just shut up—hush!

Her Excellency, Dr. Noelene Christian (United Kingdom)

FAMILY SAINTS COMMUNION

Feed us with Your Bread of Life

Like Heaven's manna.

Your springing well quenches thirst,

Reviving lost souls.

Saints' communion.

Bread of Life

Christ!

Dr. Joseph S. Spence, Sr. *(Wisconsin, USA)*

DIS YA NICE TIME!

Gungu peas and rice

Mi say man it nice

Love it wid

Guinness punch and ice

Mi Empress cook it

She just righteously wicked wid it

She put coconut milk ina it

That will mek you strong and fit

Curry goat pan di side

Dis ya dish is right in stride

Mek mi feel good inside

This stew can't hide.

A cold Red Stripe wid it lift up de spirit

Dis ya life you must inherit

Maybe a likkle Wray and Nephew

Brings out de flava of the stew

Sistren takin care a Idren

Wid dis yu mus win

Got my worl' in a spin

With the sweet lovin!'

Dr. Father T. Mosley (United Kingdom)

OXTAIL STEW BIG-UP BIRTHDAY BLESSINGS, DESRINE!

Happy birthday dear sister and gracious Desrine

May your birthday be delighted and brightly shining

We have a bowl of Jamaican Oxtail Stew for you

This dish will let you jump over the moon at high noon.

It has buttered beans and peas. The kind you liked

It is mixed with spinners, plain flour dumplings

It even has a few chochos which you liked

Not only that, it's flavored with lovely curry splashes.

The stew is brown and has a beautiful flavor but not soupy

Tasty rice and peas blended with the main ingredients

Watch this! We even throw some cowpeas in just fi yu

Included, you will love the white yam and green banana fingers.

There is also a blending of spicy seasoning—flavoring tasting.

It's all mixed up with Ital stuff from Jamaica

The Land of Wood and Water—Blue Mountain flavor!

You can't forget to add likkle scotch bonnet peppa.

You know how I love that extra kick.

This kick is more significant than an old country mule back foot.

Some dasheen to make it thick and juicy

Come sista, and share it with me, missy.

This integrational stew has to be my favourite dish

Along with some succulently nice Escovitch fish.

This dish is pure ecstasy straight from back-a-yard.

Nowhere better, mi-de-pon-de-way—mi soon come!

Oxtail is my favorite meat. When I cook it, it's so sweet.

The Oxtail meat falls off the bone.

It's so lovely, and I will take a picture on my phone.

When I take it off the heat, I can't resist! It's my favorite meat.

Happy Big-up Birthday, Blessings, Desrine. God bless you always!

Drs. Father T Mosley, Noelene Christian, Desrine Williams, and Joseph Spence (UK and USA)

MOONLIGHT SERENADE: FAMILY SHINING BEAUTIFULLY BRIGHT!

I always shine like the midnight moon
Sometimes hiding behind a cloud, I play a game
See me, catch me, and kiss me if you have the fame
One day you will see me soon.

There are times when I have different shapes
Pretty, round, brown, and sweet as grapes
You may wonder why you never see me fully
Watch this—Mi spread pon toast like grape jelly.

There are times when I am half and times quarter
Believe me. I am sweet as sugar and water
Some nights I will melt your precious heart
Have your nerves jumping from the very start.

Always look above my dear for my smiling face

When you see me, you will feel my warm embrace

I will be the shining light enhancing your earthly life

Never again will you need any sugar and spice.

You will love my pretty pearly pristine shape.

It will uplift your precious soul to higher heights

We will shine bright, and I will always be your ace

Will you step out, embrace, and kiss me tonight?

Be my family, hold my hand and walk with me always!

Dr. Desrine Williams *(United Kingdom)*

FAMILY TREE: NEVER FORGOTTEN!

Who are you, as individuals or entities?

Basics bear the mark of the roots,

Anchored in the mystery of the riches from a potter's hand,

With wind dance playing your nostrils and lungs.

Dinner table and hearth sitting out days of plenty and meager,

Hope and prayers cajoling the universe for health,

Names carrying the themes of life and its twin end,

Celebrations of sorrow and joy over time.

Games and tunes that tutors' hearts to rhyme at times of roll call,

The duties and beauty's stating a claim on lay space,

A line around a circle, up and down, triangles within squares,

The being that's rich within the compass of all.

Family is more than a unit unique,

It's the kiln that dusts crusty gold,

A glittering glow for the wellness of all,

A backpack filled with contingencies and fallback plans.

Family is fascinating, and familiar paradise relived,

Every tear shed grows the units bonding and binding,

Every giggle a deposit into cement blocks of unity,

Family is the tree that shields the harsh wind.

It's a shore awash with security bonds.

Such an esteemed heritage that pays homage to life's entries and exits.

Dr. Nancy Ndeke *(Kenya, Africa)*

DOWN MEMORY LANE!

A tower that holds the light for a latecomer,
A phone call reminding love of its importance,
A note telling the awesomeness of being missed,
A gift saved for years to meet a heart's desire.

Small tasks rendered in tender emotions often dripping wet,
A neighbor may put a razing fire off your garage,
A colleague may need some pieces of advice,
A stranger may hoist some heavy bag onto your shoulder.

But family, while functional or dysfunctional,
With its bitter dramas and outbursts,
None is known to have had a choice to have or not,
A gift must have and must keep.

A legacy of sky's bounty and mischief,
Testing our abilities to give and forgive,
To love the traitor and disloyal,
Run but stay connected for blood has no parole.

Family is the war and peace fields we navigate,

To thrive within its factory settings,

It is to thrive everywhere and anywhere,

God's grace and universal bonding, never die in vain!

Dr. Nancy Ndeke *(Kenya, Africa)*

MY FAMILY ALWAYS MY FRIENDS!

People may have left everything. But it is tough to leave one's family. Losing one's family and loved ones in an unknown world that cannot be seen and cannot touch is terrible. That is the time a person feels and knows what the meaning of family is. Some will go to the mountains, the sea, or the deep forest for peace of mind when missing their family.

When a long day passes, some will get bored. They will think, is this real peace of mind? When they live in boredom without peace of mind day after day, they will begin searching for their beautiful and missing family. It has to be this way and no other way. Nature will not always make a person's mind better.

The company of our loving family and loving friend makes our minds better in a moment. Everyone's family is their friend. They do not forget you in times of sorrow, and they stay with you in your happiness. Family is the root of our lives. They will always give us light, rain, air, emotion, shade, and love.

Dr. Mili Das (India)

The love of a FAMILY is life's greatest blessing

STRENGTHENING AND LOVING FAMILY

My family is my strength

When I face trouble

My family supports me

They give me joy and love

One day we will forget everyone

But our favorite faces will always remain

As the family in the memory of your heart

The one that loves and supports us always!

Dr. Mili Das *(India)*

MY BEST HOME

We start our journey from home

We end our journey at home

When the whole world leaves us

We come back to our own home

Slowly we go to our mother

Sleep in her lap

See your mother's lap?

It's the best home of your life!

Dr. Mili Das (India)

PJ DAUGHTER AND ME MOTHER!

Sixty-six minus 44 equals twenty-two.

This number is righteously true

Follow the sequence and don't be blue

This number shows love from me to you

Sixty-six minus 44 equals twenty-two.

One of these days, you may fit into my shoe

Looking forward to us bonding like Elmer's glue

This number shows love from me to you

Sixty-six minus 44 equals twenty-two.

Fixing your dinner, I watched you chew

I pray that your dreams will always come true

This number shows love from me to you

Sixty-six minus 44 equals twenty-two.

The number of years separating me and you

Like a rising star, you wonderfully grew

This number shows love from me to you

Sixty-six minus 44 equals twenty-two.

All along, I figured that you had a clue

I have always loved to hear your point of view

This number shows love from me to you

Now we know the numbers, and they are true

Like great people, we only need a faithfully few

This number shows love from me to you

I am so happy and delighted with the faithful few!

Dr. M. P. Spence *(Florida, USA)* **& Dr. PJ Spence** *(S. Korea)*

GOD'S GRACEFUL SEASONAL BLESSINGS!

God covered me under His blessings

A thousand miles away from the land of my birth

Praying for my family to come

I have experienced many things

Now I know all the seasons of the year.

I know and have experienced the cold seasons

The wonders I saw came upon my inward mind

When winter came, I saw my first winter snow

It was a fantastic time of grace.

God in His majestic glory

That was when I know

The wonder of wonders is higher than you, and I,

I saw the winter morning

The trees stand bare and white with snow

My family would have made it warm and not cold!

I saw the spring with buds on stems and limbs one morning

Birds were on the trees

Then tomorrow came, and leaves were there

In awe and wonders, I looked upon the trees

And know for sure there is a force greater than you and I

Evening came, and the sun reduced to dew

Then it was springtime. I saw my family's smiling faces.

And then again, I wonder about God

The one I came to know

The one I wait for His appearance

Then summer is upon us.

The heat is horrid in this concrete jungle.

The trees are like an umbrella, but you get no shades

The leaves are green and beautiful, but they don't get any breeze

Maple tree with beautiful leaves changing all summer.

We only had summer with family members

Jamaica land of woods and water

January to December is all summer

I love the doctor or hummingbirds

They hover over the flowers and sip nectar.

The horrors of the summer here

For we didn't know this kind of summer in Jamaica

The land of my birth. My land of wood and water

It was not the summers here we had back there

I even saw a squirrel peeping at me through my window

Then after this horrid heat

The fall comes with all the colors of the leaves changed.

That's when I know its fall

Oh, and then came the snow again.

My family would have made it warm and not cold!

Dr. S. B. Spence (New York)

(Winter in New York)

(Jamaican Sunshine on the Beach)

DYNAMICS OF FAMILY LOVE (ANAPHORA POEM)!

Family love is not just a simplistic word

Family love represents valid words in action

Family love calls for a sincere demonstration

Family love require duty and loving obligation

Family love is not just an inconsequential situation

Family love represents loving actions in motion

Family love expands into creating a lovely creation

Family love does not increase condemnation

Family love represents uplifting a righteous nation

Family love is strong and lasting with a significant duration

Family love lives and inspires with an everlasting salvation!

Dr. Sister Shyne *(Maryland, USA)*

Note: An Anaphora Poem begins with the same lines or phrase
The lines are constant to the end and do not change.
The subject of the poem represents images strengthening the title.
The ending line culminates the poem with solidity and stability.

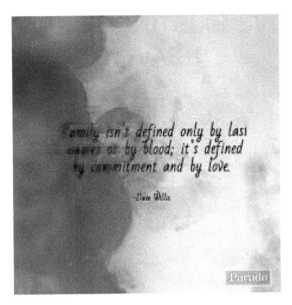

(Dynamic of the actual family)

LOVE EXISTING IN GOD'S HEAVEN!

With my respect and memory

To my dearest love these days.

My mom, my dad,

My children and my son.

I give them my honor and love to infinity

What's in my heart? They now have their home.

Like most everyone I have met and loved.

They are no more on earth!

We will meet one day in the meadows,

Where the flowers never wither.

In God's kingdom of infinity

I pay tribute to each of you who have passed on

The dearest beings of my heart

My family members, I missed you dearly

You're sitting with my dear God!

Dr. Biserka M. Vuković (Croatia)

OUR ANCESTOR'S HOUSE

We entered grandma's old house
To introduce you to my departed relatives.

The closest ones arrived
From ultra-distant spaces -
Their ethereal essence filled the rooms.
Happy, tangible, and young -
They looked over our hands,
Heard the synchronous pulsing of our hearts,
Retransmitted to us by our Creator.

A mystic ray flickered over the window,
It twisted a wreath and shone over my hair,
Another ray rose over you, over our head -
The light clothed us
We both stepped, shining
Under God's altar in Heaven.

Space music came down from the ceilings,

Our souls are exalted.

You hugged me and kissed me in front of them.

We heard my beloved ones blessed us.

We thanked them and went on our way

Sublime with the blessings of my ancestors.

Dr. Stoianka Boianova *(Bulgaria)*

PATRIARCHAL FAMILY SYNDROME

Excessive, rapid death -

The leap year

It reaped with a rusty sickle,

My root didn't miss.

My dear family, I love you!

And in the heavenly fields

It stayed forever -

For centuries the snow has been falling

On the gaping wound.

And the earth, still

Revolved, with us unquestionably,

And with cosmic sadness

We had to be human.

And the biblical goats

With warm thin-jet milk

Clarified the zodiac,

In that irresistible world.

My dear family, I love you!

Dr. Minko Tanev *(Bulgaria)*

MY PEACEFUL BLOSSOMING FAMILY!

Who is in my flowery gardens?

They live and enjoy the beats of the drums

They sing and dance with their hearts

The offspring flocks fill me with much love

While illusions emerged from my soul

It's a sweet perfume assuming equality of condition

Spring brightens—winter torrential

Summer is a bridge calling all attention.

Who are the ones that gladden my soul?

Bringing great joy and love to making me whole

When the sky is silent, and when the clouds get dark

And in summer, it does not bloom?

Oh, blessed poetry, the sweet haven of peace

Illuminate the families of the world

And in their bosom—blossom lasting peace!

Dr. Luzmila Bermudez Ramos *(Columbia, S. America)*

THE CANTAROS

The filament is pouring out

Under the blue sky

Filling the land with greatness

Sustaining family love of—Mother Earth

Oh, My God!!!

Hope is pouring out

That shelters family

When there is no moon

And there is no sun

Love waters—Mother Earth's Families.

From the floral gardens, the curtain is dressed

Mother Earth joins in with a single cry

United forever, asking for forgiveness

Our family—we will always love you

Yes sir! Yes sir!

Dr. Luzmila Bermudez Ramos *(Columbia, S. America)*

FAMILY REFLECTION—MY GREAT & DEAR BROTHER JOSEPH!

My dear, Sir Joseph, how did I deserve this honor from you?

With your love, you touched my heart, which I don't open often.

I have never had a brother and am an only child.

I have always wanted one, and then you came along.

You appeared like a genie coming out of a bottle

It fulfilled my dreams and activated my senses.

Stimulated my cognition beyond recognition

I am an artist and painter with a brush of colors.

Your soul is now forever etched in my heart.

Settle in comfortably because there is a place for you

There are no other places. You will have everything.

You transformed me into a mitochondria archetype of God's grace

I will always have a cup of Turmeric tea with antioxidant

With no sugar on the table for you to sip.

Anytime you desire to walk a barefooted mile on the beach

We will discuss the sunset while drinking some

Flavored coconut water and watching the horizon

We will dissect its true essence and sparkling sun.

My great selfless love will warm you

Water and feed our goodness and honor.

Your face will always be sprinkled with a proud smile like mine

Brilliant as the surface of a lake that reflects the environment around it.

This seal will shine forever like the morning's reflection of the sunbathing in it

My dear brother, Joseph, blessed is the day you came into my life.

Blessed are you in your life guided by the hands of God

God bless you always, my great and dear brother, Joseph!

Dr. Biserka M. Vuković *(Croatia)*

THE TENDER FAMILY BOND!

Whispering softly kissing the bloom,

Reminiscing the memories of the days bygone,

The dancing butterflies on the pretty red rose,

The moments when the lovely buzzing bees flew,

And the sparrows chuckled as the little hands spread,

To catch the fledglings running around,

Jesting, bursting with laughter abound.

The trees, the witness to the love-hate relations sweet,

Bending, swaying with gleeful smiles,

To this day, the aroma still lingers around,

Of the chatters unmindful, prompt and vague!

Though life has its ways undeciphered unclear,

With highs and lows, ups and downs,

The path unknown, with thorns and blooms,

With every twist and turn of fate,

A challenge anew, an impediment harsh.

Those days when the heart feels lonely, lost,

The perplexed mind alone when strolls,

Down the memory lane with a far stretched flight,

A soothing touch then heals the soul,

The mellifluent tunes that once we sang,

Of the warmth, of love, of the tender bond!

Giti Tyagi (India)

CROSS ROADS OF LIFE

As I sat by the window one fine morning bright,

Suddenly, I happened to find lying quietly by the bed,

A little box with a reddish violet tint and hue,

Shining sparkly as if reaching out to me,

Embedding in its breast the memories galore,

Of my loving parents and my family that I fondly missed.

Each photo reminds me of the fun that we had,

And the togetherness even in the harshest times,

The days that we spent in glee and cheer,

And those when the eyes welled up with tears.

Oh! How I miss those family dinners,

And the love-filled pots of smiles and cheers!

When on the crossroads of life I await,

As if entangled in the labyrinth of life,

I close my eyes and then fondly remember,

The loving words of my parents who embosom me forever.

The wisdom and the grace then fill my heart,

Dispelling all fears, dissipating all ignorance,

The darkness then sheds off, the distress evanesces,

With every passing moment, the bond strengthens to the core,

Comforting me, as the shade in the scorching sun,

Shining amidst the darkest clouds, the thunderous storms,

In the harshest tests of life, walking beside me, holding my hand,

Steering me through the stormy tempests, the whirlpools of life!

Giti Tyagi *(India)*

FOR MY GRANDMA...

Sowing hope,

She walks in the furrows of the earth.

With soulful words.

Many times she catches winged birds.

In search of light,

She walks through the verdant paths

With sweet smiles.

Many times, she turns stones into flowers.

In melancholy times,

She sings to remove sadness and pain.

Many times,

She stands in silence and fails to explain.

By her side, we like to cuddle,

After the long day when we are tired of our play.

Many times she says,

Stories of the pink moon she had greeted.

We touch her silky locks,

When a cool breeze ruffles her hair.

Each time she hugs,

Her warmth is never lost in the air.

On a full moon's bright beam,

Her heart understands the silence of trees.

She is my grandma,

Her heart flows like a stream.

Abode of love she is,

Her language is love.

We are her colourful butterflies,

Ready to soar over the sky and further above!

Rajashree Mohapatra (Bhubaneswar, India)

MY GRANDPA...A GREEN CRUSADER

Years passed by …

These Banyan, Pipal and Mango trees

And other more indigenous species

Are now telling us countless stories.

Our dear grandfather!

You're no less of a green crusader.

This thick foliage that you created in this village

Provides welcoming shades to weary travelers.

Oh my, Grandpa!

You have reared them as our family members.

They are thousands in numbers now.

An ultimate endeavor that you initiated over the years.

Your rare touch of affection

Have redefined compassion.

It is all for your tireless efforts

Now we all smile together.

On the bed of passing time

Your footprints are all cast fine.

You have molded thousands of minds.

No doubt, you are a gift from the divine!

Rajashree Mohapatra *(Bhubaneswar, India)*

(Grampa Green Crusader)

KNOWN AS MR. SPENCE— CLEAN AS THE BOARD OF HEALTH!

His name is Mr. Spence, and respectfully called by many

He visited my establishment, TerriLynn on Bradley

Contracted through His A Phi Brother of some wealth

His Alpha Phi Alpha fraternity brother himself came by

He wore a black tuxedo, white shirt, and black bowtie

He is known as Mr. Spence–Clean As The Board Of Health!

Many looked and wondered, "Who are those two dudes?

Making their way through the people and looking so sharp?"

They came to know him, respect him, and honor his presence

He joined the groove, made his move as a great Karaoke singer

He is known as Mr. Spence–Clean As The Board Of Health!

His advice was excellent, and a proliferator of peace and unity

He established policies and guidelines for the club's community

Those out of line, security checked them into their places

Terrilynn on Bradley operated smoothly and graciously

They shook hands and conversed with my brother at length

Known as Mr. Spence—Always Clean As The Board Of Health!

Such a classy and elegant fellow, who many started to follow

Seems like his finesse and class rubbed off, and swallowed

Smooth and sharp as a Saturday night razor blade, he stayed

Selfless, socializing, authentic, and articulate, he displayed

Known as Mr. Spence—Always Clean As The Board Of Health!

A shining and sensible star, his sophisticated presence is known

An awesome brother who stands by you through thick and thin

Always there and have time to speak about right and wrong

Knowledgeable, love Kosher food, a kindhearted kindred soul

Kept his word, a knightly armored soul who makes others whole

Known as Mr. Spence—Always Clean As The Board Of Health!

(Dr. TerriLynn Wigley, Wauwatosa, Wisconsin)

CONCLUDING PRAYER

Thank you for reading our noble and inspiring book, *International Family Poetry Anthology*. May God continually bless each one of you for your participation and in all of your endeavors. May He touch your entire body, from head to toe with His grace and mercy. May He connect every limb, joint, vein, artery, bone, muscle, cell, and fiber to work in His favor, including your thoughts, words, and deeds. May He remove every pain, negative feelings, illness, symptoms, negative invading thoughts, and the like from your mind, body, and soul. May He lead you in the path of His righteousness, dress you with His whole armor, and radiate His aura around you.

May His appreciation and commendation touch your soul and keep you whole. God didn't add another day to your life because you need it. Instead, He completed the job because your family and loved ones require your uplifting inspiration!

His words proliferate in 1 Timothy 2:1, "I exhort therefore, that, first of all, supplications, prayers, intercessions, and giving thanks, be made for all men." May He wash you over again with His love, grace, and mercy. I don't believe He brought you this far to leave you.

May God continues to shed His perpetual light upon you, your loved ones, family members, and endeavors from generation to generation.

May these words of my mouth and meditations of all our hearts be acceptable in your sight now and forever, dear God, our strength and Redeemer.

Blessings always,

Amen!

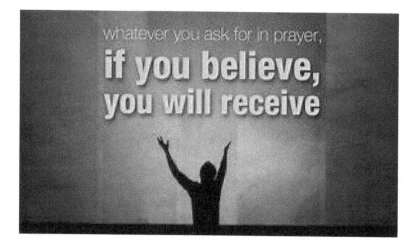

(Family members should pray inspirationally for God's blessings!)

'Tis ten years since we had a wonderful family reunion. The pandemic has been defeated with a new dawn on the horizon. The new and young Anthony to the family has caught on, and poetic love is in the air. Everyone is now hoping and praying to be the light around the table and graced in white. The family has bonded more robustly with hearts and lips, ready to tell the secret of happiness and inspirational uplifting.

Next, the phone rings, "Hello," please, when will season two be? I dare not miss this inspiring and uplifting event to come!"

Nothing is as strong as the love of family. The heart is the home where family truly resides!

Watch out for the next episode!

ONE LOVE...KEEP US TOGETHER!

Ambassador, Dr. Lovelyn P. Eyo.
Lagos, Nigeria, Africa!
International Director, Africa at Cámara Internacional de
Escritores & Artistas
Positive Thoughts Consulting & Training Solutions!

POET'S BIOLOGICAL SKETCH

Ambassador Dr. Lovelyn P Eyo resides in Nigeria, Africa. She is my dear daughter in Christ, her personal Lord, and Savior. She proliferates and manifests His spirit daily. She does not let me go too far from her and keeps in constant contact. She is a great poet and administrator. We have excellent communication, and she does not hesitate to call me if she does not hear from me. She demonstrates the essence of family, togetherness, love, respect, and ancestry for the Cradle of Civilization, the Mother Land, Africa, and the birthplace of all humanity!

Dr. Biserka M. Vuković resides in Croatia. My dear sister is an incredible artist and published author. She is very active in her artistry and poetry and has received various awards from worldwide sources for her excellence and diligent work. Moreover, she is a very trustworthy person who delivers as promised. She is an excellent writer and poetic reciter who constantly inspires her audience with words of graciousness and uplifting. She is a family person who loves her family members dearly.

Dr. Desrine Williams resides in the Jamaica, West Indies. She is fascinating and is the life of the family party. She is loved dearly by her family, is a great cook and baker of delicious cakes, which she learned from her Godfather. She is a very dedicated worker and mother. She is always ready to jump in and help wherever  and whenever she can to make the situation better. She has a luminous guiding light that assists others in getting on the right track. As a precious soul, she is into helping others. She is my gracious cousin of God's inspirational grace.

Ambassador Dr. Ashok Kumar Verma resides in India. He is a school principal, a great mystical poetic brother in Christ, an internationally recognized poet, and a great family man. Ashok is a spirited and excellent conversationalist with inspiring ideas and proliferates God's love for  humanity. He has a precious family, and they are always eager to speak with me during our conversation. He has received numerous poetry awards for his recitals and writings, and his poetry style is admired by many worldwide. He is my dear brother in India.

Dr. Giti Tyagi resides in India. She is an editor, creative artist, award-winning international trilingual author, poet, book reviewer & translator. She has master's degrees in English, Education, and Philosophy and holds a UGC-NET certificate. She is a former senior  lecturer from MM University, Ambala, India, and an educational consultant at Karnal, India. She has won several appreciation awards for teaching and was honored, in 2019, for her contributions to the literary world. She is the author of - *Priceless Pearls, Crossroads & Other Stories, and The Ascent of A New Dawn.*

Dr. Gloria Antoine resides in Maryland. She started her teaching education and practical teaching experience in Jamaica, West Indies, where she attended and graduated from St. Joseph's Teachers College. Upon immigrating to America, she obtained a degree in biology and  secondary education as well. She retired as a teacher and returned to teaching as a substitute teacher. After her final retirement, she volunteered as a teacher to help children. She resided with us as a great family member in Jamaica. Her dad was the best barber in town, who cuts our hair every month. Gloria is a pleasant person and is loved by many.

Dr. Katherine Stella resides in Wisconsin. She was born to Italian and German parents and the second to five boys and five girls. She entered the United States Army after high school. She worked in Minnesota law enforcement and retired with thirty-one years of service. She  wrote poetry with Poetry Alliance Group, UK. Many poets took her under their wings, like Pat Farnsworth Simpson and me. Her book is "Time For Haiku." She turned many poems into songs, which has earned gold and platinum recordings.

Dr. Kathirina Susanna Tati resides in Malaysia. She is the patriarch of her Family, proliferating much love for them. She was born in Kota Kinabalu, Sabah, Malaysia. She has written nine books consisting of novels for adults and children, a collection of short  stories, poems, folklore stories, and drama scripts for Radio Sabah. Three of her novels are translated into English. She also organized twelve anthologies, short stories, and poems amongst Malaysian writers. She was twice awarded the

Sabah Literature Awards for the years 1996/1997 and 2016/2017. Besides writing, Kathirina also actively participated in singing her Kadazandusun ethnic songs and poems.

Dr. Luzmila Bermudez Ramos lives in Santa Marta, Magdalena, Columbia, South America. She is a remarkable poet who runs her poetry site "Comunidad Literaria De Lectores Pájaros Del Alma" (Literary Community of Readers Birds for the Soul Columbia). This group consists of active poets worldwide. The most recent event sponsored by the group is the "Nelson Mandela Poetry Recital," which had laudatory comments and sponsorship from many. Some of her videos are on https://www.youtube.com/watch?v=sfrrQ12U9UQ and recitals on https://soundcloud.com/luzmila-bermudez-ramos.

Dr. Manjula Asthana Mahanti resides in India and graduated from Bareilly College with post-graduate studies from Allahabad University. She retired as a schoolteacher and senior lecturer from KPRC Kala Kendra, Bareilly University. She is an inspirational poet with many awards, author of several poetry books, and conducts many recitals, which is an ongoing tradition in India's poetic legacy. Her recent book is "Manjula's Potpourri: Treasure Trove of Emotion." She is a Hindi translator and also travels frequently to recitals to enhance her skills

Dr. Marsha P. Spence resides in Florida, USA. She is a mother, sister, cousin, niece, a great friend to others, and the Most High God's inspirational child. She processes and demonstrates dynamic faith in her personal Lord of Savior, Jesus Christ, and is a

dedicated steward in His vineyard. She loves her family, stays in communication, is a dedicated vegetarian, natural juice mixer, and exercises regularly. Additionally, she maintains diligence over her health and God-given human temple with much grace. Her personality is very uplifting, and there is never a dull moment in her graceful presence.

Dr. Mili Das is an extraordinary poet, does many recitals, and is an excellent personality in India. In addition, she is the prolific author of two poetry books in English published in America, studied at Rabindra Bharati University, is married, and has two great children. She is a judge on television cooking shows, appears regularly as a guest on Rupashi Bangla TV and Zee Bangla Rannaghor Show. Additionally, she is a regular recipe writer at Sangbad Pratidin News and appears on Zeal Sports and Onkar News TV.

Dr. Minko Tanez resides in Bulgaria and lectures in Bulgarian for international students at the Medical University, Plovdiv. He authored six Bulgarian poetry books and co-authored two Indian bilingual haiku poetry books. He is a published author in anthologies and editions worldwide. Listed in European Top 100 most creative haiku authors and World's Best Poets Anthology, "Temirqazyq" 2019. Co-author of "Songs of Peace," the World's Biggest Poetry Anthology 2020, he is published in "Atunis Galaxy Anthology" 2021, the first, second, and the third anthology of "World Gogyoshi," and "World Haiku" 2015-2021. He is awarded for the "First World Poetry Competition of Newspapers and Televisions" China, 2020, and has numerous awards from literary societies.

Dr. Nancy Ndeke resides in Kenya. She is my clairvoyant sister of God's inspirational grace, who has kept my feet from dashing against stones during my travels. She is a great author of several inspirational poetry books and one of the best poets whose verses I have ever read. She is genuinely family orientated and loves her  family members dearly. The essence of her life is deeply rooted in God's grace and redemption. Her most recent anthological publication is "Save Africa." Consisting of poets from across the Mother Land continent and Cradle of Humanity. She is a retired school teacher who uplifted her students educationally and reverently with God's inspirational grace and loving mercy.

Dr. Her Excellency Noelene Christensen resides in the UK. She is a very inspirational servant in God's vineyard. Her thoughts are uplifting and progressive. She is a grandmother, cousin, daughter, and niece. You name it, whatever is inspirational and uplifting—she  is it! She is a blessed soul proliferating Christ's inspiration and beautification to worldwide humanity in real-time and online. She is truly blessed with God's reverence and love and is one of my most fantastic cousins from childhood. Thus, she acquired the title of Her Excellency!

Dr. Paulette Spence-Hines resides in Jamaica and lectures for the School of Tourism Hospitality and Entertainment Management at Excelsior Community College. She completed her training in Drama and Education at Edna Manley College of Visual and Performing  Arts. She has a Master of Science in workforce education and development from the University of Technology. She is an

117

international Tour Guide Trainer who spent over ten years in tourism training with other Caribbean countries. She is an Elder for Portmore Moravian Church, serves on various committees, and plans to publish a poetry book.

Dr. Professor Carla F. Spence is an attorney-at-law who resides in South Korea. She teaches English and Spanish to Korean scholars, has a great time with her students, and enjoys learning their language, history, and customs. She is a world traveler who studied in Spain, Dominican Republic, Canada, the U.S.A., and other places. She is highly motivated, inspirational, knowledge-seeking, and has many existential questions. She professes Christ as her personal Lord and Savior. She loves her Family with much dedication and is an uplifter of living life to its fullest in God's grace.

Dr. Rajashree Mohapatra resides in Odisha, India has received a master's degree in History, Journalism and Mass Communication from Utkal University, Odisha, and is a professional educator. She is a post graduate scholar in Environmental Education and Industrial Waste Management from Sambalpur University Odisha. She is a dedicated social activist for the cause of social justice, environmental issues and human rights in remote areas through non-governmental organizations. Poetry, Painting and Journalism are her passions which she proliferates with awesome inspiration to worldwide humanity.

Dr. Sandra Y. Spence resides in Jamaica. She graduated from the University of The West Indies, Mona Campus, with a BA Ed (Hons). She is a senior literary specialist at T. Dip Green Pond High School, Cornwall Courts, Montego

Bay, Jamaica. She is very uplifting, motivating, inspiring, progressive, and a dedicated professional educator. Her most favorite inspirational quote is, "Education breeds confidence. Confidence breeds hope. Hope breeds peace." – **Confucius.**

Dr. S. B. Spence resides in New York, USA. She is a professional nurse and is dedicated to her career. She loves the New York environment and the quality of life it has to offer. She is active with political activities in her neighborhood and dedicatedly assists her political representatives. She loves to travel and is a very inspiring conversationalist. She is a mother and grandmother who loves her family very dearly. She stays current with medical advancements and is very adaptable to emerging changes and improvements in her area of nursing practice.

Dr. Sister Shyne lives in Maryland, is a natural and organic food consumer. Creates and blends natural juices. She is my eldest daughter, and we had great times at Fort Campbell, KY. She truly loves and will never forget the great delicacy her grandmother Olive Spence cooked, and she was ready to eat after coming home from school. She is the published author of *Out of Darkness into Light. The Price of Redemption by Sheritta X.* Radio Show, Host/Producer of "Another Clean Glass Production & The Sisterhood Connection." "The Original Man Hour." "Women of the Scriptures Right Down to Modern Times," is an Artist Management, and Creator of a Natural Hair & Skin Care Products.

Dr. Sonni Ramirez lives in Maryland, USA. We had a great time when we lived together in Ft. Campbell, Kentucky military base. She is my dear daughter. My mother lived with us back then. All of the children loved her cooking, especially Sonni. They would hurry home from school in the evening to have some of their grandmother's unique and flavored cooking with natural spices. Her favorite drink was cool Sorrel with ice cubes, especially in the summertime. She always has a great smiling face.

Dr. Stoianka Boianova lives in Bulgaria, has a master's degree in physics. She has authored twelve poetry books, novels, and short story books published in Bulgaria. Co-authored two bilingual haiku poetry books, India; "Songs of Peace," the world's most significant poetry anthology 2020; The world's first, second, and third anthology "Gogyoshi." Published worldwide and ranked in European Top 100 most creative haiku authors, and world's best poets, "Temirqazyq" 2019. "World Haiku" Anthologies, 2015-2021. Awarded for the "First World Poetry Competition of Newspapers and Televisions" China, 2020, and received numerous global literary awards.

Dr. TerriLynn Wigley resides in Wauwatosa, Wisconsin. She is a community business advocate known by the people. She operates TerriLynn's Soul Food Express Restaurant. Taught Sunday School and received many Trail Blazing Awards from community organizations and governmental figures. She continuously studies dietary skills and enhancements in college and has applied her intuition in

many fascinated ways to uplift South Eastern Wisconsin with delicious delicacies and extraordinary dining events.

Dr. Tony Father Mosley resides in the UK. He served in Her Majesty's Navy. Dr. Mosley is a grandfather. He loves his Family and abides by his Empress's wishes. He is the best DJ in the UK. His "Soup & Dumpling  Show" is broadcast midweek and weekends on TGM Radio to worldwide multicultural humanity. *He is a Jamaican linguist with an international audience* of the arts and programs with a long-lasting difference in the world's social and environmental future.

ABOUT THE ORGANIZER: DR. JOSEPH S. SPENCE SR (EPULAERYU MASTER)!

Bio Narrative: Amb. Prof. Dr. Joseph S. Spence Sr, USA
(Epulaeryu Master)!

His Excellency, Honorable, Ambassador, Professor, Commissioner, Dr. Joseph S. Spence Sr, USA, (Epulaeryu Master), is a prolific author of eleven poetry books. In addition, he is an intellectual educator, worldwide award-winning poet, and creative reviewer of over 50-books posted in multilingual pedagogic mediums. He is a recipient of worldwide accolades, resides in Wisconsin, provides advocacy to many, and assists worldwide humanity.

He authored over 200 scholarly peer-reviewed articles in various genres, with over 200,000 inquiries on this link: https://ezinearticles.com/expert/Joseph_Spence,_Sr./194051. His first book, "A Trilogy of Poetry, Prose, and Thoughts for the Mind, Body, and Soul," was a best-seller. His second, "Trilogy Moments for the Mind, Body, and Soul," won the Best Christian Poetry Award. His third, "The Awakened One Poetics," won 2nd place in Critters Writers Workshop Best Author's Pool and the publisher's best-seller, and his tenth is "Sincerely Speaking Spiritually."

In addition, he received many military awards for his honorable career as a field-grade commander. His military comrades named him "Apollo," the Greek mythical god of poetry and music, for his poetry writing skills and recitals. He has traveled the world and inspired humanity with his electrifying poetry. His poems have been published in twenty-one languages, and he speaks and translates in four languages.

As the co-founder and poetry chaplain of the Worldwide Poetry Alliance, he has donated one hundred percent royalty from five books he published with the Worldwide Poetry Alliance. The royalties were donated to charities that assisted 911 first responders with medical care, who helped the injured in the terrorist's aircraft attacks on the World Trade Center and Military Pentagon. He also co-authored the "World's Biggest Poetry Anthology: Songs of Peace," published in March 2020.

He retired from the US Army as a decorated field-grade commander. Governor Bill Clinton (42nd USA President) appointed him as a Goodwill Ambassador, Arkansas, for assisting students at the University of Little Rock, Arkansas, entering graduate school and helping local citizens meet their perceived goals. He received the Outstanding Poetry Student Award from the English Department, University of Wisconsin, Milwaukee, where he serves as a "Lead - The Change Agent" and is a Literary Thought Leader for Golden Key International Honour Society.

He has served in various poetry leadership positions, including: an Advisor for the World's Parliament of English Literature-India, Global Advisor for Global Literary Poetry-India, and advisor for Renascimento Millennium III Renaissance Together for Europe-Egypt. He is a USA Independent Poet Laureate and has received numerous global poetry awards for his published poems and articles. His writings and poetic verses are published in: Spanish, Japanese, Chinese, Polish, French, Scottish Gaelic, Korean, Swahili, Filipino, Hindi, Assam, Bengali, Arabic, Italian, Croatian, Vietnamese, Orissa, Jamaikan Potwa/Patois, and Rastafarian languages. He resides in Wisconsin, USA.

MORE BOOKS TO ADD IN THE CHECKLIST WRITTEN BY THE AUTHOR

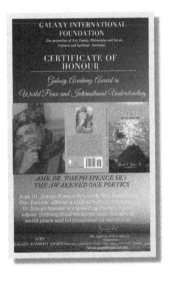

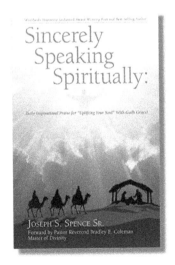

Printed in the USA
CPSIA information can be obtained
at www.ICGtesting.com
LVHW091144050124
767941LV00063B/2183